# Dear Parent:

Congratulations! Your child is tak... the first steps on an exciting jour... The destination? Independent read...

**P9-EGN-718**

**STEP INTO READING®** will help your child get there. The program offers five steps to reading success. Each step includes fun stories and colorful art. There are also Step into Reading Sticker Books, Step into Reading Math Readers, Step into Reading Phonics Readers, Step into Reading Write-In Readers, and Step into Reading Phonics Boxed Sets—a complete literacy program with something to interest every child.

## Learning to Read, Step by Step!

**Ready to Read    Preschool–Kindergarten**
• big type and easy words • rhyme and rhythm • picture clues
For children who know the alphabet and are eager to begin reading.

**Reading with Help    Preschool–Grade 1**
• basic vocabulary • short sentences • simple stories
For children who recognize familiar words and sound out new words with help.

**Reading on Your Own    Grades 1–3**
• engaging characters • easy-to-follow plots • popular topics
For children who are ready to read on their own.

**Reading Paragraphs    Grades 2–3**
• challenging vocabulary • short paragraphs • exciting stories
For newly independent readers who read simple sentences with confidence.

**Ready for Chapters    Grades 2–4**
• chapters • longer paragraphs • full-color art
For children who want to take the plunge into chapter books but still like colorful pictures.

**STEP INTO READING®** is designed to give every child a successful reading experience. The grade levels are only guides. Children can progress through the steps at their own speed, developing confidence in their reading, no matter what their grade.

Remember, a lifetime love of reading starts with a single step!

Published in the United States by Random House Children's Books, a division of Random House, Inc.,
1745 Broadway, New York, NY 10019, and in Canada by Random House of Canada Limited, Toronto.

Step into Reading, Random House, and the Random House colophon are registered trademarks
of Random House, Inc.

Visit us on the Web!
StepIntoReading.com
randomhouse.com/kids
dckids.kidswb.com

Educators and librarians, for a variety of teaching tools, visit us at
randomhouse.com/teachers

ISBN: 978-0-375-86898-6 (trade)—ISBN: 978-0-375-96898-3 (lib. bdg.)
Printed in the United States of America    10  9  8  7  6

STEP INTO READING® STEP 2

DC SUPER FRIENDS™

# CRIME WAVE!

By Billy Wrecks

Illustrated by Dan Schoening

Random House New York

People are lining up
to see the world's
biggest pearl.

Aquaman cuts the ribbon
to open the show.
Superman, Batman,
and all the people cheer!

Suddenly, water floods in.
The people exit.

The Super Friends

help the people.

Tentacles rise

out of the water!

It is a giant octopus!

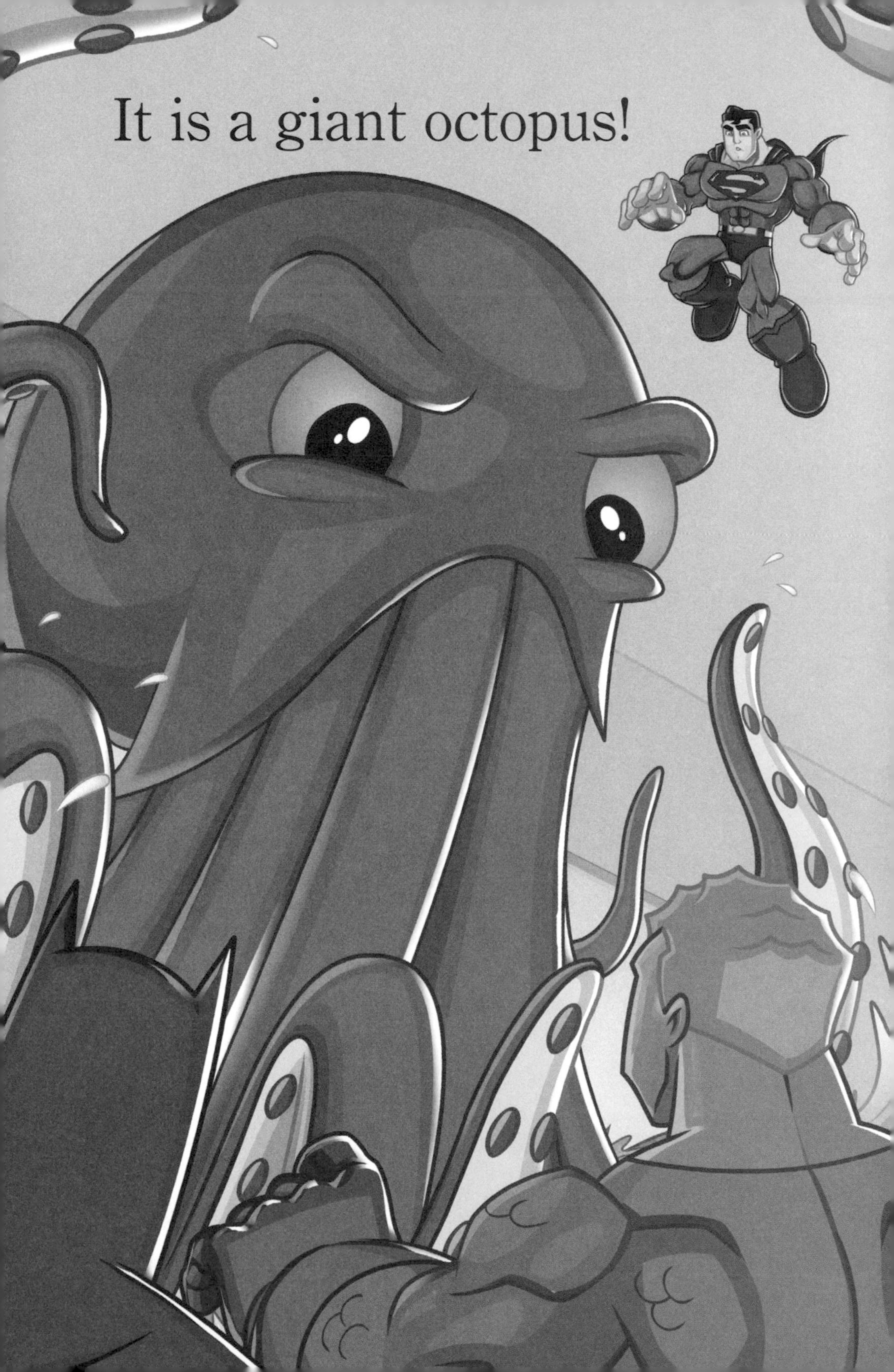

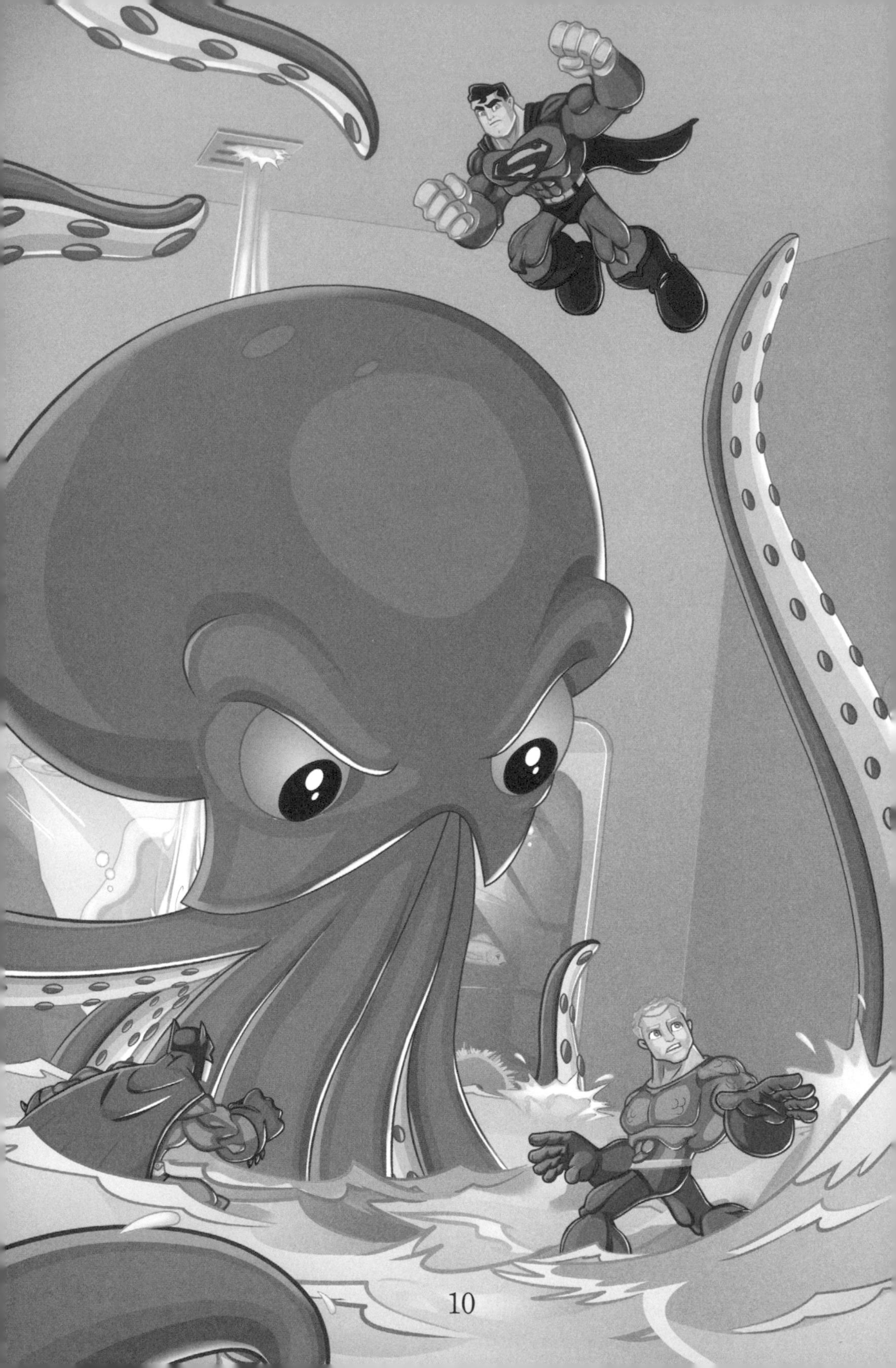

Black Manta rides a
shark into the room.
Electric eels spark
around him.

Black Manta
picks up the pearl.

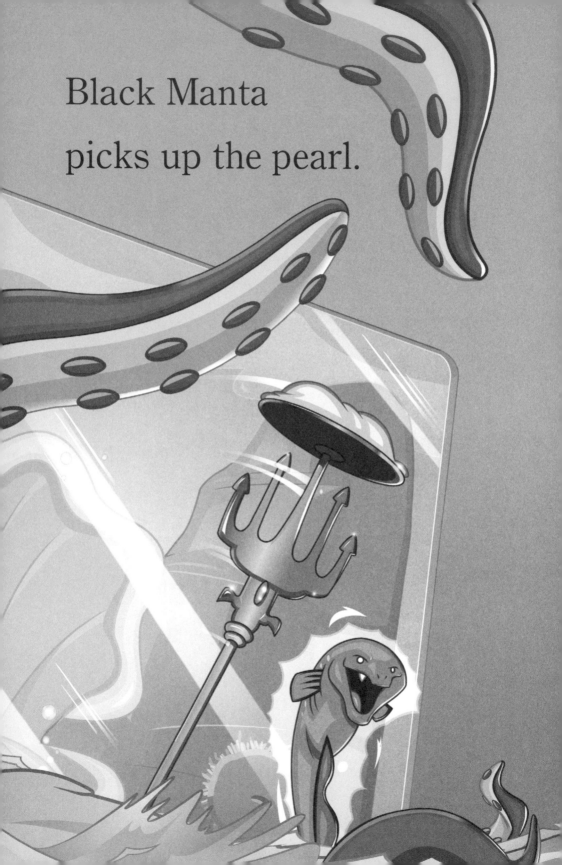

He is stealing it!

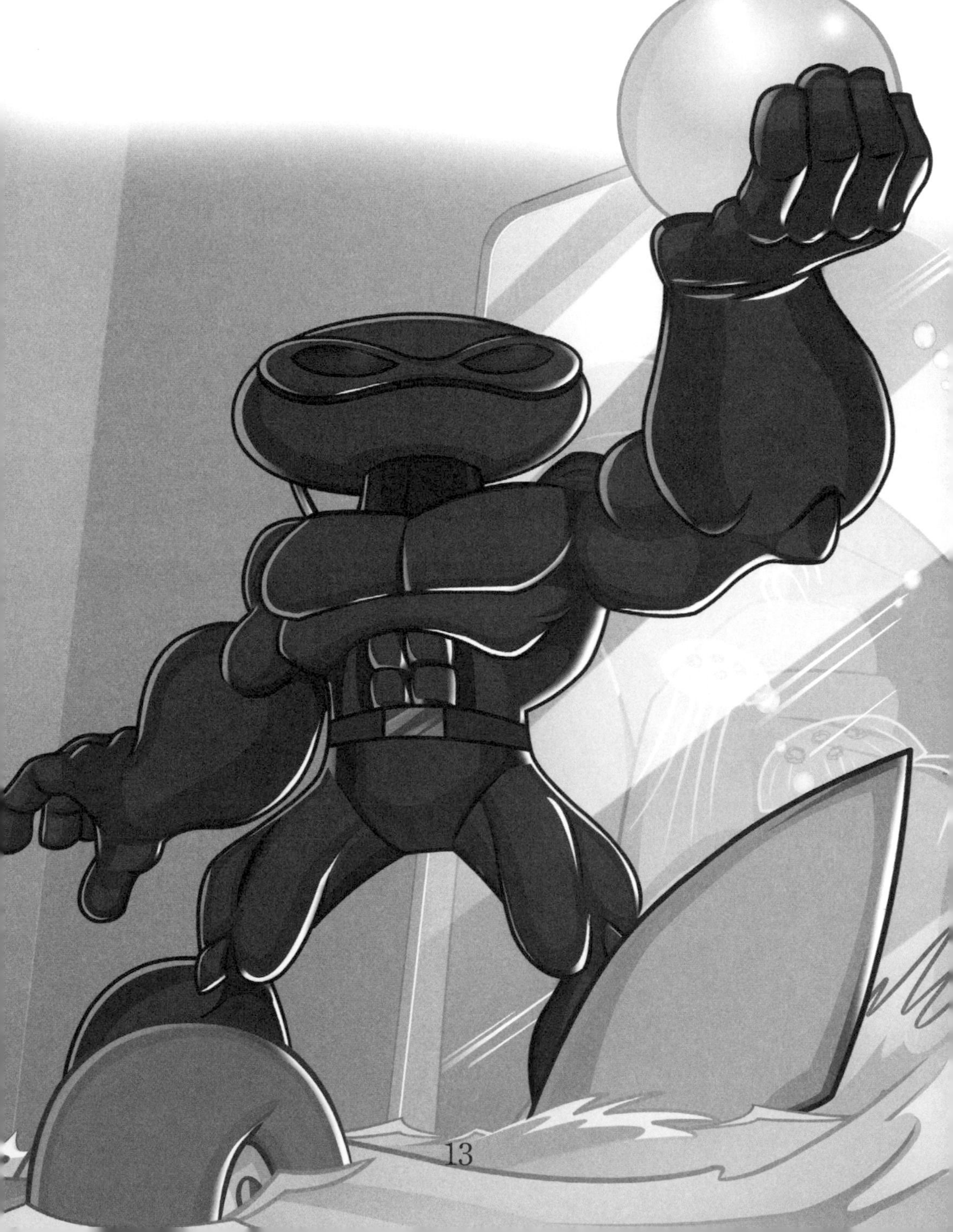

The Super Friends stand
in Black Manta's way.

They will not let him
take the pearl.

Black Manta gives orders.
The shark, eels, and
octopus attack
the Super Friends.

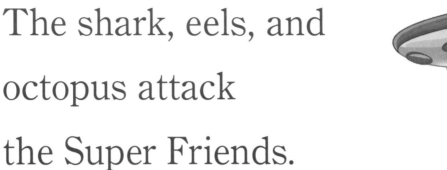

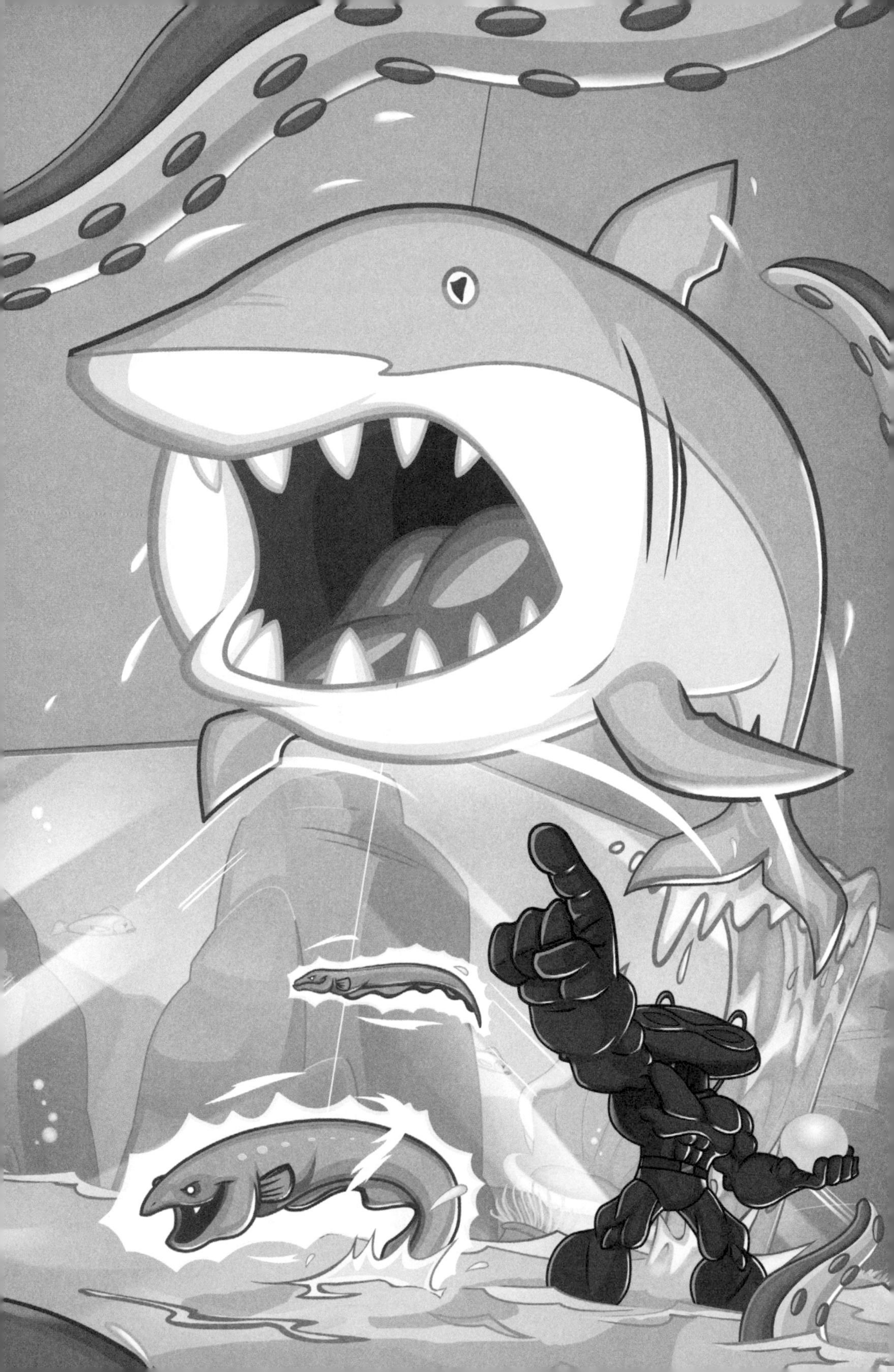

The electric eels
chase Batman.
He swings toward
the penguin pen.

The water is freezing.

The eels trap Batman!

The shark snaps
at Aquaman!

Black Manta clutches
the pearl.

Superman fights
the octopus.

Black Manta

blasts Superman

with his lasers!

"I have won,"
Black Manta says.
"The pearl is <u>mine</u>!"

He forgets that Aquaman
can talk to sea creatures.

Aquaman tells
the octopus
that stealing is wrong.

The octopus sets
the Super Friends free.

Black Manta
falls backward.
A giant oyster clamps
down on his foot.

Black Manta is trapped.

Batman gets the pearl.

The police take

Black Manta away.

Batman and Aquaman put the pearl back.

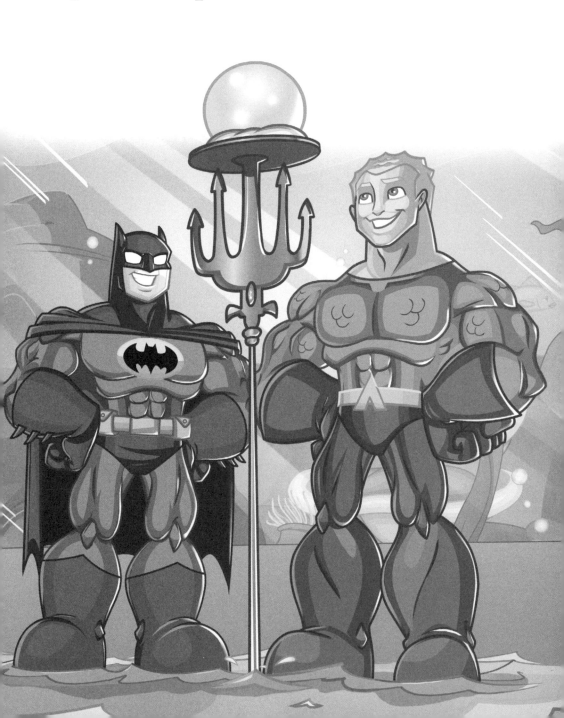

"I'm glad you are
on our side,"
Aquaman says.
"We don't have enough
Bat-Cuffs to arrest you!"